BILLY SLATER
PRESENTS
SHOW
AND GO

A Random House book
Published by Random House Australia Pty Ltd
Level 3, 100 Pacific Highway, North Sydney NSW 2060
www.randomhouse.com.au

First published by Random House Australia in 2014

Addresses for companies within the Random House Group can be found at www.randomhouse.com.au/offices

National Library of Australia
Cataloguing-in-Publication Entry

Author: Loughlin, Patrick.
Title: Show and go / Patrick Loughlin, with contributions from Billy Slater; illustrated by Nahum Ziersch.
ISBN: 978 0 85798 268 1 (pbk)
Series: Billy Slater; 3.
Target Audience: For primary school age.
Subjects: Rugby League football – Juvenile fiction.
Rugby League football players – Juvenile fiction.
Other Authors/Contributors: Slater, Billy; Ziersch, Nahum, illustrator.
Dewey Number: A823.4

Illustration and design by Nahum Ziersch
Typeset by Midland Typesetters, Australia
Printed in Australia by Griffin Press, an accredited ISO AS/NZS 14001:2004 Environmental Management System printer

Random House Australia uses papers that are natural, renewable and recyclable products and made from wood grown in sustainable forests. The logging and manufacturing processes are expected to conform to the environmental regulations of the country of origin.

SHOW AND GO

WRITTEN BY
PATRICK LOUGHLIN

ILLUSTRATED BY
NAHUM ZIERSCH

RANDOM HOUSE AUSTRALIA

BILLY SLATER

As a fullback, there are times when I go looking for the ball and there are times when I rely on other players to feed me the ball when my side is attacking. Similarly, my teammates depend on me to be there to back them up if they make a break. Being fullback also means my team has to trust that I will do my very best to stop the opposition from scoring. It's an awesome feeling when your team believes in you, and this helps me to be a better player.

Rugby league is a team sport, and being a good team player is the most important quality a footballer can have. Some of the most successful set plays require the whole team to be involved, and quick passing between players can allow your team to get past the opposition. Plus, it's fun to get everyone in on the action!

In *Show and Go*, you will read about how Corey, one of the best players on the West Hill Ravens Under 11s team, becomes fixated on scoring more tries than anyone else. Corey, however, soon comes to the realisation that being a ball-hog is no fun.

I hope you enjoy reading *Show and Go* and understand that you can't do everything yourself on the footy field. Great players are selfless and do whatever they can to help their team win.

Billy Slater

Corey Wilson was running. Not on a footy field, but up a hill.

Despite the fog, Corey recognised the place. *Everyone* knew the hill on Patterson Drive. The local kids called it The Big Dipper. Joggers called it Heartache Hill.

Corey knew the hill from helping his mum drag a shopping cart of catalogues up it each fortnight. But why was he running up the hill now – and in his Ravens football gear? He also couldn't work out why, no matter how far he ran, the top of the hill wasn't getting any closer. The harder he ran, the further the top of the hill seemed to be.

But that wasn't all.

Through the fog, he could see another player running ahead of him. The figure soon pulled away and the fog closed in. Corey stopped running. He was all alone at the bottom of the hill.

With the radio playing.

Corey opened his eyes to a darkened room. He squinted at the clock radio on his bedside table. It was 5.30 am. *Time to get up.*

The clock radio used to be in his mum's room, but sometimes she was so tired she

would just sleep through it. So Corey was now the one who had to get up first.

Corey stumbled through the dark hallway and into his mum's room.

'Mum,' he mumbled.

Nothing.

'Mum!'

'What? Oh. Right,' his mother said groggily, scrunching her eyes and yawning. 'Cattledogs?' she asked.

'Cattledogs,' confirmed Corey.

The cattledogs were the shopping catalogues they delivered in order to stay on top of the bills. Corey had once mispronounced them as 'cattledogs', and that's what his mum had called them ever since.

Corey's mum had always done it hard when it came to money. She had always done it alone, too. Corey's dad had left when Corey was only a few months old. Since then, it had just been Corey and his mum.

When they sat down to eat breakfast, Corey's mum tried to lighten the mood.

'Big game today?'

'I suppose.'

'Isn't it the Kingsville Crushers?'

'Destroyers,' said Corey, rolling his eyes.

'Oh, right. That's what I meant. They're pretty good, huh?'

'They're the reigning premiers. They beat us in the first round.'

'I'm sure, with you out there, the Ravens will get them this time,' said his mum.

Corey sighed. 'I dunno. We've got a lot of pretty hopeless players on our team.'

'That's a bit harsh. What about Liam? And Junior? He's good. And what's his name? The fullback.'

'Cameron?'

'Yeah. He's fast, isn't he?'

Corey snorted. 'I'm faster.'

'I'm just saying you shouldn't put down your mates.'

'They're not my mates,' grumbled Corey.

'Hopefully we can get the cattledogs out of the way quickly and get you to your game nice and early. You know what they say – the early bird gets the . . . something.'

Corey rolled his eyes again.

'What time did you say you start?'

'Nine o'clock,' said Corey.

'Right, we better get moving then. Hurry up and finish your toast. Only five hundred to deliver today.'

Five hundred catalogues to stuff in letterboxes on a Saturday morning. Corey suddenly remembered his dream. He didn't usually remember his dreams. *Maybe this one means something*, he thought to himself.

By the time the game against the Destroyers was over, he would be having that thought all over again.

Corey and his mum got to the West Hill Ravens homeground twelve minutes before kick-off.

'Corey! Where have you been, mate? We were getting worried,' said Coach Steve. 'Quick, get your boots on and head out there. The boys are doing a final warm-up.'

'Good luck, honey!' Corey's mum said a little too loudly.

Corey winced and ran onto the field.

'He's a really good kid,' said Corey's

mum, and Coach Steve nodded politely.

Corey's mum always came to his home games because the ground wasn't too far from their apartment. But ever since their rusty blue sedan had broken down, she rarely made it to the away games. They were still saving up to get it fixed.

THOOOWEEEEEP!

At exactly 9.02 am the ref blew the whistle to start the first half.

Corey was fired up and ready to go. No one would ever guess he had spent the early morning delivering catalogues. When it came to footy, there was something that burned white-hot inside Corey. He was a natural. Spectators who saw him play often said so. It didn't matter if they were Ravens supporters or supporters of the opposition, they all seemed to agree.

Corey knew it, too. In fact, he felt it. His mum didn't talk much about his dad, but she did say that he had played rugby league. His mum said she had loved watching him play. 'He could have played first grade if he wasn't such a hothead,' she had told him once. Maybe that's where Corey got his talent from. Wherever it had come from, Corey never doubted his own ability. The second he stepped on a football field, it felt like he was home.

His natural ability, speed and confidence had made him the Ravens top try-scorer. Unfortunately, it had also made him the least liked player.

'Tai, pass it out here,' called Corey, despite the fact it was only the second tackle and Tai, the Ravens five-eighth, was giving big Junior Taafuli a tackle-busting run up the centre of the field.

Come on, thought Corey. *Give me the ball. We've got to beat these guys!*

Corey hated losing and he really hated losing to the Kingsville Destroyers. They had been the top team ever since he started playing footy four years ago. In that time, the Ravens had never beaten them. He was starting to get sick of seeing the Destroyers do their little victory dance. But it wasn't just about the Destroyers.

Whenever Corey got the football and started running, it was like everything else faded away. It didn't matter that his dad wasn't around, it didn't matter that his mum couldn't pay the rent. When Corey had the ball, he was in control. He could do anything. He could weave and dodge and beat the defence. He could run fast and strong, all the way to the tryline. He could win the game for his team.

So when he got the ball two tackles later, that's exactly what Corey did. He'd been watching his opposite number on the Destroyers team rush up early in the attack, and it wasn't that difficult for Corey to time a quick sidestep past the centre and find a gap. Suddenly, he was away, and it was time to put the foot down.

Turbo time, he thought to himself, and kicked his legs into overdrive. He left the rest of the Destroyers' defence for dead, with only the fullback left to beat. It was time for his trademark show and go.

He had Josh Brown, the Ravens left wing, backing up on the outside. Josh had improved in the last few rounds. He was quick, too. Corey could time the off-load just right to commit the fullback to the tackle and let Josh race away to score. *But why let Josh take all the credit? Best to stick with the plan. Show and go.*

Corey waited until the fullback was upon him. All he had to do was throw a well-timed dummy to Josh, wrong-foot the fullback, turn back on the inside and then sprint to the line and put the ball down under the black dot. Simple.

But when he threw the dummy to Josh, the fullback didn't flinch. Instead, he threw himself at Corey as if he'd known Corey's plan all along.

THUMP!

Corey's back hit the ground, and the fullback landed on top of him. To make matters worse, the ball came loose and went rolling away for the chasing Destroyers to regather.

'You are *so* predictable,' said the Destroyers fullback. He pushed himself up from the tackle, using Corey's face as support. 'You did *exactly* the same thing in the first round.'

'Oh,' gulped Corey. He'd never been called predictable before.

The Ravens Under 11s were completely unprepared as the Destroyers turned defence into attack. A few quick passes and, suddenly, it was the Destroyers who were scoring under the black dot of the goalposts, making for an easy conversion.

It was 6–0 to the Destroyers.

Corey was once more at the bottom of the hill.

'I don't even know what to say after that performance,' began Coach Steve.

The team sat in silence. It didn't matter whether Coach knew what to say or not, he was bound to say something anyway. And after they had lost 36–6, it was bound to be bad. Very, very bad.

'Yes, the Kingsville Destroyers are good. And, yes, I guess you could say we got destroyed today. But what's even *worse* than getting beaten by a good team is getting beaten by yourselves,' said Coach Steve.

Here we go, thought Corey. *Lecture City.*

'I think we self-destructed today,' Coach continued. 'Why? Because we didn't play as a team.'

Corey suddenly felt all eyes on him. 'Why are you looking at me? I was the only one who scored!'

'Because you're a hog! You never pass it,' said Josh, glaring at Corey.

'Maybe I'd pass it more if you knew how to back up better,' replied Corey.

'I *was* backing up. You dummied twice instead of passing to me,' said Josh.

'He's right, Corey. You blew at least two tries because you held onto the ball,' said

Liam. 'The Destroyers were onto you, they knew you wouldn't pass it. That's why your dummies don't work anymore.'

'But I . . .' Corey began, but the words of the Destroyers fullback were ringing loud and clear in his ears like a car alarm.

You are so *predictable.*

'But I . . .'

'Scored? Yeah, we know. From an intercept on our tryline. You got lucky. If you'd missed the intercept, it would have been 40–0,' Liam stated bluntly.

Corey looked around the change shed for a friendly face, but the players who weren't staring at him in disgust were either shaking their heads or looking away.

'That's enough,' said Coach Steve. 'The loss isn't all Corey's fault. So the intercept was risky, but it worked. And Corey may need to vary his play more, but there were thirteen of you out there. Corey wasn't the only player running one out or not helping his teammates in a tackle. If you boys don't learn to play as a team, we have no chance of making the semifinals.'

There was an awkward silence. Junior looked down at his boots. Azza clicked his tongue. Josh cleared his throat, and Corey just stared straight ahead.

'Do we have a chance of making the semis, Coach?' asked Liam.

'I need to have a look at the table after this, but I think so,' Coach replied. 'But we can't afford to keep losing like this. Luckily, I don't have any hair left or I'd have been tearing it out today.' He looked at the glum faces around him. 'Come on, lads, it's not all bad. We just have three games left of the season. Let's make them count, hey?'

'We will if someone passes the ball more . . .' mumbled Cameron.

'Hey, that's enough,' said Coach Steve, but the damage was done.

'Maybe we just need a better fullback – someone who can actually tackle,' said Corey. He slammed his gear into his bag and stormed out of the change shed.

‘Something wrong, Cor?’ his mum asked as they walked home. ‘You seem angry.’

‘Nope.’

‘Don’t worry, you’ll beat the Destroyers next time,’ she said cheerfully.

Corey stopped walking and threw his bag down. ‘No, we won’t. We never beat the Destroyers. And while I’m playing in this stupid team, we never will!’

‘You know, I think you are a little angry. Don’t you have an appointment with Mr Timms at school next week? Maybe you need to talk to him about how you feel,’ suggested his mum.

Corey imagined sitting in the school counsellor’s office and telling him about his feelings. He snorted a hot breath of air, then kicked his bag clear across the footpath.

4 ANGER ISSUES

Mr Timms smiled a wide, friendly smile. ‘So, Corey, how’s your mum going?’

‘Dunno.’ *How is Mum*? It wasn’t something he thought about often. ‘Okay . . . I guess.’

‘She’s a good mum. She’s done it pretty tough, hasn’t she?’ asked Mr Timms, but Corey knew it wasn’t meant as a question.

Corey shrugged and looked around the office. There was a collection of Smurf figurines on a shelf and some hand puppets hanging from a hook. One puppet, a smiling brown dog with a big red tongue, had the word 'happy' printed on its collar. The other puppet was a boy wearing a T-shirt with the word 'sad' on it.

On the wall was a poster of a cat dangling from a tree branch. The caption underneath it read 'Hang in there'. That poster always bothered Corey. Just how long *does* that cat have to hang in there? *It looks like it's been hanging there for a while . . .*

'So, Corey, how are *you*? Have you been having any more of those angry feelings?' Mr Timms smiled a slightly concerned smile this time.

Corey thought for a moment about what had happened in the change sheds after Saturday's game.

You're a hog. You never pass it.

Cameron's words bounced around his brain like a pinball. Corey could feel his ears tingling and his cheeks burning at the memory of it. Then he thought about his mum asking him if he was angry. *Why is everyone always asking me that?*

Mr Timms looked at him expectantly. 'Corey? Anything you want to talk about? We could use the puppets if you like.'

Oh, no. Not the puppets again. Corey bit his bottom lip. He could tell Mr Timms about how Cameron and the rest of the team had blamed him for the loss, even though he'd been the only one to score a try for the Ravens. But then Mr Timms would ask more questions.

‘Not really,’ Corey said finally. *So what if I’m angry? My teammates are idiots. What is so bad about being angry, anyway?*

‘You know, there’s nothing wrong with feeling angry. It’s a completely natural feeling,’ said Mr Timms.

How does he do that? wondered Corey. *It’s like he’s a mind-reader or something.* ‘Yeah, I know,’ he said, staring at the cat poster.

‘Considering that’s it just you and your mum at home, you may find you feel angry sometimes.’

Corey looked at Mr Timms. ‘Why?’

‘Well, not having a dad around can be hard for young boys like yourself. Sometimes that can make you feel a bit upset and you may take that out on others.’

'But I hardly even remember my dad,' said Corey. 'Why would I get upset over someone I don't even know?'

Mr Timms smiled at Corey again, but this smile was different. It was the smile you get when someone feels sorry for you. Maybe he should have just told Mr Timms about what Cameron and his teammates had said. That's why he was angry – not because his dad wasn't around.

Corey glanced at the clock. *How much longer?* For once he found himself wishing he was back in class.

'Corey, remember the first time you came to see me last year?' asked Mr Timms.

'Yep, I got in trouble in Ms Cooper's class.'

'Do you remember why?'

'For throwing my chair at the smart-board,' Corey said in a voice that made him feel like he was five years old.

Why was Mr Timms bringing this up? His mum had yelled at him for a week. He'd spent three whole days in detention. According to one sixth grader, that was a school record.

'Do you remember why you threw your chair at the smartboard?' Mr Timms asked softly.

'No,' said Corey.

Except he did remember. It had all begun when Corey had refused to make a Father's Day card. When Ms Cooper suggested he make one for his mum instead, Corey had screamed at her and thrown his chair at the board. The principal had threatened to make his mum pay for the damage, but in the end she didn't have to.

Mr Timms looked at Corey with his usual smile of encouragement.

'Can I go now?' asked Corey.

'You can if you want to,' said Mr Timms.

Without a word, Corey got up and left, grabbing a handful of jellybeans from the jar on Mr Timms' desk. At least it hadn't been a complete waste of time.

'Come back and see me anytime,' said Mr Timms, but Corey didn't hear him. He was already halfway down the hall.

That afternoon Corey braced himself for the death stares he was expecting to receive at footy training. But when he arrived at the ground, he found Josh sitting by himself.

'Hey, Corey,' said Josh. He was hunched on the bench, tying a shoelace.

'Hey.' Corey threw his bag to the ground. 'Where is everyone?'

'I think they're stuck in traffic. There was an accident on Harley Road. You didn't see it?'

Corey thought about his mum's broken-down car sitting in their driveway. 'Nah, I legged it.'

Josh nodded, then looked around. 'So . . .'

Corey suddenly realised he'd never had a proper conversation with Josh before. 'So you still think I'm a hog?' He'd never been very good at holding his tongue.

'Um . . .'

Luckily, they were saved by another arrival.

'Hey, where's everyone else?'

Josh turned to see Junior, and smiled with relief. 'Stuck in traffic, I think.'

'Well, I'm not going to waste my time waiting around for them,' Corey said, skulking away in a huff.

'What's his problem?' asked Junior.

Josh shrugged. 'Same thing as always.'

Junior shook his head and laughed.

Corey heard the two boys talking but resisted the urge to turn around. He kicked at the grass, then sprinted off to the end of the field.

When the team finally got on the field, it didn't seem any different to any other training session. Was Corey the only one who remembered what had happened after the game on Saturday?

'Come on! Get those knees up, boys!' barked Coach Steve, as the team ran some sprint drills. 'Good work, Cameron. That a boy!'

What? thought Corey. *I'm the one who's leading!*

'That's it, Ravi. Good running!'

What a joke – he's coming last! Corey was running rings around everyone, but Coach Steve didn't seem to notice.

Later, as the boys waited in line to practise passing, Corey couldn't help himself. When he saw Josh drop a pass he had to say something, even though the pass had been from Ravi and was way over Josh's head. 'He can't even catch a pass. How can he expect me to let him score a try?'

As soon as he said it, Corey wanted to take it back.

‘What do you mean “let him score”?’ said Cameron, who was standing directly behind Corey in the line.

‘Just that, you know, if I pass it and –’

‘You really think you’re the best player on this team, don’t you?’ said Cameron.

‘I’ve been top try-scorer for two years in a row,’ Corey said defensively.

‘You’re not as good as you think, Wilson. You’re just a ball hog. I’m only two tries behind you, and there are three games left. I bet you *I’ll* be top try-scorer by the end of the season.’

Corey looked at Cameron’s face. He was deadly serious. ‘You don’t stand a chance, Cotter,’ said Corey, but something inside him was wobbling like jelly. He didn’t like the idea of a bet for top try-scorer, but he didn't want Cameron to know that. 'What do I get when I win?' Corey said, trying to sound confident.

'A year's supply of pizza!' shouted Tai. He and a few other Ravens were now watching the challenge unfold.

Junior shook his head. 'You need to get over this pizza obsession, dude.'

'I like pizza,' said Tai.

'I don't,' said Cameron. 'How about . . . an annual pass to Big Wave Fun Park? It opens in November and I want to be first in line.'

There was no way Corey or his mum would ever be able to afford an annual pass to Big Wave Fun Park. 'Bring it on, Cotter. You'll never be top try-scorer, anyway!'

'Ooooh!' said the boys around them.

Why did I say that? thought Corey. *I can't afford that pass.*

'It's on!' said Azza.

Cameron held out his hand and Corey shook it. 'No backing out,' said Cameron.

'Not a chance,' said Corey.

He would just have to make sure he won. All he had to do was score more tries than Cameron in the next three games. He'd been leading try-scorer all year. How hard could it be?

'Get ready, Wilson. You're going down!' said Cameron, his grin as wide as a goal-post.

Corey simply shook his head, but inside the jelly was wobbling again. There was no way out now.

WHR
WHR
WHR
WHR

6 JUST THE TWO OF US

Corey walked up the footpath to his apartment block. His nose was running, his mouth was dry and his legs were throbbing from the run home in the cold. He just wanted to crash on the lounge and forget about the bet he'd made with Cameron Cotter.

As he walked up the stairs, the smell of curry punched his nostrils. 3B had been at it again. Corey's stomach grumbled as he opened the door to 2A.

This apartment was the third they had rented in two years. Each place seemed to be getting a little smaller. His mum called it downsizing. 'It's cosier to have a small place when it's just the two of us,' she'd said when they'd moved in.

As Corey stepped into the empty apartment, it felt anything but cosy. It was near freezing. He could put the heater on but Corey knew his mum would worry about the power bill, so he pulled his hoodie over his head and walked to the kitchen. He glanced at a note that was stuck to the fridge door.

Corey switched on the oven and took the box of fish fingers out of the freezer.

At least the oven would help to warm up the room.

'Corey, I'm home. Did you eat dinner?'

Corey forced his eyes open. 'Yeah,' he said groggily, from beneath the blanket.

'Oh, good. Guess what? I picked up an extra shift tomorrow!' His mum paused, looking guilty. 'The bad news is you'll have to deliver the cattledogs by yourself.'

Corey groaned.

'I'm sorry, Cor, but we really need that extra money. You'll be right, won't you?'

Corey didn't respond. His eyes were glued to the TV. Smiling kids were zipping down giant waterslides to a catchy pop song. 'Ride the biggest wave this summer at Big Wave Fun Park,' commanded the voiceover. 'Opens November.'

'That water park is opening soon,' said his mum. 'With this overtime and the catalogue money, we might be able to go. What do you reckon, Cor?'

Corey would have groaned again but his throat was locked. 'Maybe.'

The image on the TV disappeared with a soft blip. Then the lights went out.

'Not again! I'm sure I paid the power bill this month.' Corey's mum sighed. 'I'll get the candles. You find the matches.'

This time Corey did groan. *Could things get any worse?*

Of course they could.

7 CATTLEDOGS AND SUVs

The next afternoon, as Corey dragged the shopping cart of catalogues along Paisley Parade, he was feeling a little better about life. His mum had called the power company first thing in the morning and had managed to get the power restored. And even though he was delivering cattledogs – and would be for the next two hours – at least the weather was good.

It was a sunny winter's day with a light breeze that made it feel like spring. The pleasant weather meant he could stuff the catalogues into people's letterboxes without his fingers going numb. On a really cold day there was nothing worse than trying to separate the catalogues and roll them up when he couldn't even feel his hands.

Corey was almost at the end of his fifth street and the trolley was already feeling lighter. He probably needed to pay closer attention to all those letterboxes with the 'NO JUNK' stickers on them, but Corey would explain to anyone who complained that the Crazee Bargains catalogue had so many super deals it was more a community-service announcement than junk mail. Besides, the more mailboxes he skipped the further he had to walk.

It had taken Corey much less time a few months ago, when he'd had a skateboard. That was another thing his mum had promised to buy him, just as soon as she got ahead of all the bills. 'Maybe for your birthday,' she'd said.

Corey would believe it when he saw it. He knew his mum did her best – she worked so hard to make ends meet – but the ends seemed to just get further and further away.

Perhaps that's why he loved footy so much. Scoring a try didn't cost a thing. Well, besides registration fees and footy boots and mouthguards. *Guess that's why I'm delivering cattledogs*, thought Corey. *Could be worse, someone from the team could see me.*

It was at this exact moment that Corey

noticed a shiny black SUV coming up the street. Corey knew that car from footy training. The boys always went on about how cool it was. His worst fears were confirmed when he saw a familiar face sitting in the back seat. Those fears became a nightmare when the SUV's left indicator started blinking. Corey quickly ducked behind a hedge just as the SUV pulled into the driveway next door.

He peered through the hedge as a picture-perfect family stepped out of the sparkling SUV. Cameron Cotter's perfect family.

Their house was huge, with two storeys, a satellite dish, solar panels and a double garage. *Typical*, thought Corey. *I bet there's a pool in the backyard, too.*

Cameron's mum was tall with blonde bouncy hair. She looked like she had just stepped out of a shampoo commercial – not tired and blotchy, the way Corey's mum looked after a hard day at work. Mrs Cotter had perfectly applied make-up, wore a designer tracksuit and not a single strand of her hair was out of place.

Cameron's younger sister was a mini clone of her mum, except her hair was in a bun and she was wearing some kind of ballet outfit. With her long neck and pointy upturned nose, she looked like a ballerina. She leapt out of the car and began to twirl.

Then there was Cameron. When Corey saw him, he could feel his ears tingle as if all the blood had rushed to his head and

was trying to escape through the tips of his ears. Cameron had his head down, absorbed in some game on his phone, and there was a large smirk on his face. Corey knew that smirk. It was the smirk Cameron gave when someone congratulated him on a good tackle or a try. Corey hated that smirk.

The garage door began to lower, and Cameron's shiny black SUV and perfect family slowly disappeared.

At least they didn't see me, thought Corey. He grabbed the trolley and popped out from behind the hedge, ready to make a quick escape down the street.

'Wilson? What are you doing in my neighbour's hedge?'

Corey froze. *Think quick. Say something clever.* 'Nothin'. What are you doing?'

'I live here,' said Cameron.

Corey mentally kicked himself. *Stupid brain.*

Cameron pointed to the trolley full of shopping catalogues. 'So you're the one who keeps putting all that junk mail in our letterbox. I didn't know you had a job.'

'What? Yeah. Nah. I found this . . . on the way home from school,' Corey said sheepishly. 'I'm just going to chuck them in the creek. You know . . . for fun. Want to come?'

'Um, no. That sounds lame.' Cameron turned to go, then stopped. 'Maybe you should just deliver those things, anyway.

You might make some money to pay for that Big Wave pass you're going to owe me in three weeks,' he said, his smirk returning.

'Whatever,' Corey squeaked with less attitude than he wanted.

Cameron shrugged then disappeared into his perfect two-storey house, and Corey was left cursing himself on the Cotters' driveway.

Things had definitely got worse.

Saturday came and, with it, Round Twelve. There were just three rounds left of the season. At 8 am, Corey stood outside, waiting for his ride to the game against the Willamurra Wolves.

A few minutes later, Coach Steve pulled up in his dusty old station wagon and gave a friendly wave. Coach always made sure Corey had a lift to the away games. If another parent couldn't take him, he drove Corey himself. Lately, it seemed as if fewer parents were willing to give Corey a lift to the away games.

Corey waved to Coach, then ran back inside. 'I'm going, Mum!' he shouted up the stairwell. He ran back out without waiting for an answer.

Corey's mum soon appeared on their tiny balcony. 'Good luck, Cor! Score one for me!' she yelled, waving. She often said that before a game, and Corey would usually reply with 'No worries'. Today, though, he didn't feel so sure.

When they arrived at the ground, Corey helped Coach Steve carry the jerseys, half-time oranges and training balls to the change sheds. The other players trickled in a few at a time, and everyone was buzzing when Billy Slater walked into the room.

It didn't matter how often the team saw their famous mentor, it was still exciting to have a living legend of rugby league standing right there in front of you. The whole team crowded around him noisily until Coach Steve gave a loud whistle.

'All right, boys. Listen up. Billy's taken time out to be here today because it's the pointy end of the season. Three games left and they are all must-wins. Billy's going to be watching you guys and looking for anything we can work on at training this Tuesday. So show him what you can do!'

shouted Coach Steve. 'Billy, did you want to say a few words to the team?'

'Sure.' Billy cleared his throat. 'Okay, guys. As Steve said, I'm here to check out your form and hopefully give you a few tips. One of the best things I can tell you right now is to play as a team. Steve says you didn't perform so well last week, but if you're going to win the next few games and have a shot at the semifinals, you have to play for each other.'

As Billy was speaking, Corey could feel the eyes of the other players slowly settling on him. Corey turned to see Cameron smirking. Cameron bounced his eyebrows up and down and mouthed the words 'BIG WAVE'. Corey rolled his eyes.

'Oi, you should be listening to this,' Coach Steve whispered sternly.

Corey turned his attention back to Billy. He resolved then and there that, once he got out on that field, he was going to outplay Cameron and turn that annoying smirk of his upside down.

'Come on, Willamurra! These Ravens have got nothing!'

Corey looked over at the large red-faced man yelling from the sideline. Things were not going to plan.

At the start of the second half, the Ravens had been up 10–0. But now, thanks to a strong easterly wind at their backs, the Wolves were clawing their way back into the game. They had just scored a rather soft try straight through the middle of the

Ravens pack. To rub salt into the wound, Corey had to watch Cameron score one of the Ravens' two tries off a brilliant grubber kick from their captain, Liam McGill.

The other try had been a great solo effort from Liam, burrowing through the Wolves' tryline defence like a mouse through a crack in the wall. There was no doubt that Liam was having a blinder. Corey, on the other hand, felt like someone had poured concrete in his boots. He just didn't seem to be able to break away from the Wolves defenders. Now that the Ravens were running against the wind, it would be even harder.

Corey looked at the scoreboard: 10–6. They had to stay ahead, their season depended on it. And *he* had to score a try.

He needed to keep his two-try buffer. He just had to choose the right play. The perfect moment.

With nine minutes left on the clock, Corey saw that moment. Not an intercept like last week but a penalty. He just had to convince Tai to trust him. The Wolves had been penalised for being inside the five. Tai usually took the kicks for touch, so Corey ran straight over to him before he had the chance. 'Forget the kick. Cut-out pass,' he said in Tai's ear.

'What? Are you crazy? We're forty metres out from the tryline!' said Tai.

'The kick won't go anywhere in this wind. Play the quick tap and give us a cut-out pass out wide. They won't be ready for it. They'll be waiting for Junior or the twins to take it up the middle.'

Tai shook his head at Corey like he was crazy, but he trusted Corey's instincts. 'Okay, but don't blow it,' he relented. 'We need this game.'

'I won't!' Corey said as he got back into position.

Liam, who was standing further out the line, raised his hands in question. Tai just shrugged, then shocked everyone by taking the tap.

Corey was right – it was all about timing – and Tai timed it to perfection. He shaped to pass to Junior, who was steaming in on his right, then turned a complete one hundred and eighty degrees and torpedoed a long, drifting pass over the heads of the Ravens

forwards and into the waiting hands of a galloping Corey.

Corey didn't waste a second. He side-stepped two Wolves defenders and pierced a hole through their defensive line like a rocket through the clouds.

Then he was away. Legs pounding. Heart thumping. Blood rushing to his head.

The line was open but the cover defence was closing. He had two players to beat – the winger and the fullback. All he had to do was show and go.

You're a hog. You never pass it. Cameron was in his head again. *You just don't want me to win the bet*, thought Corey. *But this is* my *try.*

The wind picked up. Corey could feel himself slowing down, pushed back by the wind. The tryline looked further away, like the top of Heartache Hill. *Not now!*

Corey looked to his left. He found a wide-eyed Ravi Rangarajan running behind him, struggling to keep up.

Oh, great! The worst player on the team.

Corey was slowing. The wind was too strong. The fullback was on him.

We need this game.

What choice did he have? He could just take the tackle. If he could time the pass and Ravi actually caught it, he could eliminate the winger, get the ball back from Ravi and still score. *I just have to get the pass right. It could work.*

But as soon as the ball left his fingers, Corey knew he had forgotten something.

The wind. It blew the pass backwards behind Ravi. The Wolves winger snapped up the ball and ran away down the sideline. With the wind behind him and the wing undefended, no one could catch him.

Corey could barely watch as the Wolves winger stormed over the tryline to score, giving the Wolves the lead.

Corey had just lost the Ravens the game. Their season was over.

'Well, boys, the good news is the season isn't over.' Coach Steve grinned at the Ravens Under 11s, who were gathered for their training session. 'We still have a shot at the semis.'

'How, Coach? I thought we were out of the running,' said Liam.

'As you know, only the top five teams go through to the semifinals,' Coach Steve explained. 'However, the way the table is stacked, we might scrape into fifth place.'

'Woo hoo!' shouted the boys.

'Don't get too excited. We have a chance but nothing's certain,' said Coach. 'In fact, where's our statistician? Ravi, what were you telling me before?'

Ravi Rangarajan may not have been the best at footy, but when it came to maths, he was a whiz. 'We are currently in sixth place,' he began, looking very serious. 'After examining the win-loss ratios of the other three teams at the bottom of the table, and calculating the probability of the results of the final two rounds, we have a thirty-nine per cent chance of ending up in fifth position.'

How about you calculate the amount of time you warmed the bench this season? thought

Corey. He would normally share a smart-alec remark but, after his performance on Saturday, he felt it was best to stay quiet. He hadn't stuck around after the game to listen to the rest of the team bag his performance. He could imagine what had been said. For the first time in his life, Corey hadn't even wanted to come to training. But he couldn't risk Coach sitting him out for the next game. He still had a bet to win.

'Thanks, Ravi,' said Coach. 'That's why today's training session is really important. Luckily, we have our secret weapon here to help us . . .'

Billy stepped forward and gave the team a wave. 'By the looks of those clouds, we may need to get a move on,' he said, motioning to the black sky overhead.

For the next hour the team worked hard. They followed Billy's and Coach Steve's instructions, even as the wind picked up and the first large drops of rain began to fall. Billy gave each of the boys advice on how to improve their game. He helped the backs work on their cover defence and showed the forwards how to twist out of tackles and off-load the ball for second-phase plays. The thing Billy wanted them to remember most of all was to always follow the play and support the man with the ball.

'You can't just think about yourselves out there, you have to work together,' said Billy. 'Think of the team as a centipede. You guys are the legs. If all the legs are moving, the centipede can go forwards. But if a pair of legs stops –'

'The centipede trips over!' Tai shouted excitedly.

'I was going to say it stops, but trips over works, too.' Billy laughed. 'So let's keep the centipede moving forwards.'

'Okay, last drill before it buckets down, boys – Hot Potato,' said Coach Steve. 'One

line, quick passes, no one drops it. Let's see how many hands we can get through in a minute!'

As the Under 11s formed a line, Corey stood back and rolled his eyes.

He'd gone along with the other drills, even though he'd heard it all before. He could see the same players making the same mistakes. *Now we have to play this silly game.*

As soon as Ravi or Josh get the ball, they'll drop it. What's the point?

'Come on, Corey! Get into gear, mate!' said Coach Steve.

Corey rolled his eyes again, then jogged into line. *Fine, I'll show them fast.*

As the drill began, each player on the team passed the ball to the player on his left, then sprinted to the end of the line to keep the chain going. Corey stood at the end, next to Azza.

As soon as the ball hit his fingertips he sprinted away out of the line. *Turbo time!*

He didn't even look as he passed the ball off to his left. The ball hit the ground a metre in front of Liam's feet, and the whole team groaned.

'Thanks a lot, Corey,' said Liam.

'What? I didn't drop it!' protested Corey.

Liam shook his head, and Corey knew what he meant. His pass had been terrible.

As if on cue, big fat raindrops began to fall. Coach Steve looked up at the grey clouds rolling over them. 'That's it, boys. See ya Saturday!' he shouted.

'Bye, guys!' said Billy. 'Good work today. You smashed it!'

The boys ran off to the car park and into warm, dry cars – all except for Corey. He stood in the centre of the field, the rain pelting his skin.

He'd got it wrong again.

11 A RIDE HOME

Corey wasn't sure how long he'd been standing in the rain. In a way, he didn't care. What did it matter how wet he got? He would just have to walk home in the rain, anyway. Besides, he liked the rain. It made him feel numb.

Then he saw something big and bright approaching. A large gold umbrella. 'Corey? You okay?'

Corey felt a sting of embarrassment.

Billy got to where Corey was standing

and looked around. He stuck his hand outside the umbrella. 'Hmm. You do realise it's pouring?' he joked.

'Don't care,' mumbled Corey.

'Need a lift home?'

Corey looked down at his feet.

'Can any of your mates give you a ride?' asked Billy.

'They're not my mates,' said Corey. 'They all hate me.'

Billy gave Corey that same smile Mr Timms had given him. 'Come on, Coach will give you a ride home.' Billy held out the umbrella and waited. Reluctantly, Corey stepped under it.

For the whole way home, Corey sat silently in the back of Coach Steve's station wagon, watching the raindrops explode against the windowpane.

Coach looked at Corey through the rear-view mirror. 'So I'm dropping you off at home, then I'm driving Billy back to his hotel. Reckon I could become a professional chauffeur?'

Corey remained silent.

Coach Steve looked over at Billy and shrugged.

'Hey, Corey, I was watching you on Saturday,' said Billy. 'You have a mean right sidestep. Just remember, you don't want to overuse it in a game.'

Corey nodded but his eyes were fixed on something outside his window. He didn't speak until they approached his street.

'You can just drop me off at the corner,' he said.

'Don't be silly! It's cats and dogs out there,' said Coach Steve.

Most kids would be thrilled to have Billy Slater come to their house but Corey couldn't think of anything worse. They pulled up at his apartment block, which looked even more miserable in the dim glow of the streetlight. 'Thanks for the lift,' he said, trying to make a quick getaway.

'Is your mum home, Corey?' asked Coach Steve. 'Maybe I should tell her we dropped you off. She might be worried.'

Corey shook his head. 'She's probably still at work. She always is.'

'Will you be okay?' asked Billy.

'I'm fine. I can take care of myself, you know!'

Corey got out of the car and ran up the wet path to the apartment. 'Who needs them, anyway?' he muttered.

But the sour, uneasy feeling in his stomach seemed to disagree.

12 I CAN MAKE IT

When Corey arrived at the Ravens homeground that Saturday, there was a buzz of excitement and energy in the team. They had already formed a circle on the field, happily following Coach Steve through a series of warm-ups.

Coach Steve had funny names for all the exercises. Instead of Star Jumps, the team did Disco Jumps – along with disco moves that always made the boys laugh. There was also Crazy Legs, which involved running as fast as you could on the spot and pulling crazy faces.

Corey looked at the smiles of his team-mates and frowned. He didn't feel like joining in.

'Off you go, Cor. Good luck, love,' said his mum.

'Thanks,' Corey muttered. He slowly trotted over to the team, who were now passing the ball around.

'All right,' said Coach Steve, 'who's ready for a big game? Is Blake?' Coach fired the ball to Blake.

'Yes, Coach!' replied Blake, passing the ball back with gusto.

'Is Poppa?' Coach asked, flicking the ball to his right.

'Yes, Coach!' said Poppa, snapping up the tricky pass and throwing it back.

'What about . . . Matthew?' called Coach, tossing the ball behind him.

'Michael,' Tai corrected.

Matthew 'Michael' Miller leapt up and caught the footy. 'Yes, Coach!' he yelled, hurtling the ball back.

'Jackson?' asked Coach, but was drowned out by a loud 'Woooo!' from Junior and Tai, in their best Michael Jackson impersonations. All the boys giggled.

'Yes, Coach,' replied Jackson, laughing so hard he could barely pass straight.

'Very funny,' said Coach Steve. 'Okay, who else? Oh, here comes . . . Corey!' He threw a long pass to Corey, just as he was joining the circle. Corey took the pass easily and rocketed the ball back without saying a word.

'Okay, then,' said Coach Steve. 'Guess you call that silent but deadly.'

A few of his teammates chuckled. Corey could feel all their eyes on him again. *Who cares what they think?* he told himself. *Just make sure you score more tries than Cameron. That's all you need to worry about.*

But when the game started, that proved to be easier said than done. The Ravens were up against the Burnsfield Bears. If they won today, the Bears could also keep their season alive, and they were determined to make it happen.

Their defence in the first half was nothing short of amazing. Even big Junior Taafuli found it hard to bust through their line. Twice, when Junior had rumbled through the middle and looked like off-loading, he was smothered by Bears defenders.

But the Ravens were determined, too. The tips Billy had given the backs on cover defence were put to use. Both Cameron and Jake combined in a tackle right on the tryline to keep out a near-certain try. Jake tackled low and Cameron wrapped himself around the ball to stop the Bears' enormous second rower getting the ball down. Then Nick Raco pulled off a great sliding tackle to force the Bears winger over the sideline.

At half-time the score was still 0–0. Coach Steve was happy with the team's commitment to defence, but all Corey could think about was crossing the tryline before Cameron did. He just had to figure out how.

The answer came midway through the second half. As the game wore on and the forwards began to tire, Corey saw an opportunity. And with barely a breeze to slow him down, he liked his chances.

Until now, Corey had been following Billy's advice and had refrained from overusing his right sidestep. He had either run straight or stepped off his left all game. But this time, when Liam gave him a quick cut-out ball, Corey dummied left and stepped back in on his right. The slow-moving Bears' defence fell for it, and Corey darted through the gap.

He powered down the field like an Olympic sprinter. He could hear the defenders behind him and he could see the Bears winger moving across in cover defence. Only one thought ran through Corey's mind: *I can make it.*

As the winger reached him, Corey stepped off his left and got around him.

I can make it.

With twenty metres to go, Corey glanced behind. To his right, the Bears' speedy fullback was gaining. To his left, Cameron was giving chase.

He wants my try, thought Corey. He sped up. *I can make it. I'm almost there.*

'Corey!' yelled Cameron. 'I'm open!'

Ignoring him, Corey prepared to launch himself at the tryline. *I can make it.*

The Bears fullback lunged for his legs. Corey felt a slap against his right ankle, and his body stopped dead. Then he fell – half a metre short of the line.

He lay on the ground as the Bears fullback completed the tackle. Unable to move. Unable to breathe. Unable to . . .

'Get up and play the ball, Corey! Quick!' screamed Cameron. He ran over and helped Corey to his feet.

Corey managed to play the ball while Cameron easily evaded the few Bears defenders who had got back to the line in time. Corey watched as Cameron crossed to put the ball down under the posts. *My try. He stole my try.*

The rest of the Ravens cheered. They

ran over to their fullback and hugged him in celebration. Corey stood, rooted to the spot, stunned.

Though the Ravens won the game 4–0, Corey couldn't help but feel cheated. He and Cameron were now on equal tries for the season. The top try-scorer would be decided in the final round. And so would the winner of the bet.

13 YOU GET WHAT YOU GIVE

'Everything okay?' asked Billy.

Corey looked up from where he was sitting, in the shadows behind the floodlight. It was the following Tuesday after the game, and he'd come over here to be alone. 'I'm fine, just taking a breather. That all right with you?'

'Um, sure. You just seemed a little . . . *angry*.'

There was that word again. Why does everyone always think I'm angry? 'Nope. I'm fine,' Corey said through gritted teeth.

'Oh, right.' Billy smiled. 'It's just that when you dropped that pass, then swore and booted the ball off the park, you seemed angry. Good to know you're all right. I'll just leave you here to sulk in the shadows.'

Corey turned his face away, but he couldn't help smiling as well. 'I'm not sulking. I'm–'

'Fine. I know,' Billy said with a chuckle. 'But if you *were* angry at something, you wouldn't have to tell me. You could always just say, "Billy, I have a stitch" and that could be code for being angry. But you're not, so . . .' Billy turned to walk away.

Corey swallowed and took a breath. 'Billy, I have a stitch.'

'I wouldn't worry,' Billy said, turning around. 'It'll go away in a minute.'

Corey snorted, but this time it was a snort of laughter.

'What do you think caused this stitch?' asked Billy. 'Too much water during the break?'

Cory looked up at Billy. 'I made a really dumb bet.'

Billy raised an eyebrow. 'Oh, yep. That'll give you a big stitch. What was the bet?'

'I bet Cameron that I would score the most tries this season,' Corey said with a sigh.

Billy nodded. 'Let me guess, since you made this bet, tries have suddenly become a lot harder to score?'

'Yeah. How did you know?'

Billy tapped his head. 'Your brain – it's a powerful thing in footy. In all sport, really. Overthinking things can get in the way of *doing* them.'

Corey nodded. 'It's all I think about.'

'You know, I had almost the exact conversation with Josh in the first few rounds,' said Billy. 'He just wanted to score *one* try, though.'

'Oh.' Corey suddenly remembered how he had made fun of Josh every time he'd dropped a pass. *Why did I do that?*

'Why do you want to be top try-scorer?' asked Billy. 'Besides winning the bet.'

Corey thought about this for a moment. 'I guess I just like scoring tries. It's that feeling when everyone is cheering for you. It's like I'm someone . . . special. It doesn't matter where I live. It doesn't matter that I never see my dad. All that matters is that I scored.'

Billy looked down at Corey and smiled. Not a 'Gee, I feel sorry for you' smile, but a smile that showed he understood. 'It *is* a great feeling,' he said. 'Is that why you don't pass the ball much?'

'I . . .' Corey began to protest but stopped himself. 'Maybe.'

'I've played with – and against – many amazing players, and a lot of the greatest players I've known weren't the ones who scored all the tries. The great players are the ones who aren't trying to be great. They're not looking to be heroes or number-one try-scorers. They do whatever they can to help their team win. Great players are selfless.'

Corey nodded. He knew the players Billy was talking about. Players who worked their guts out, who tackled all day and never gave up. They never stopped trying, even when they were beaten. He'd thought he was one of those players. Until now.

'I guess, like life, you get what you give,' Billy continued. 'Don't be afraid to give something, mate. You may be surprised by how it makes you feel.'

'I'll try,' said Corey.

Billy nodded. 'How's that stitch?'

'Gone,' Corey said, a grin spreading across his face.

'Told ya,' said Billy. 'They always go away eventually.'

14 HEARTACHE HILL

Corey stared at the shopping cart loaded to the brim with the latest Crazee Bargains catalogues. Then he looked up at the mammoth hill in front of him. Heartache Hill.

It was Thursday and, once again, Corey was delivering them by himself. He and his mum always struggled to get that cart to the top of the hill. It would be near impossible doing it alone.

After his talk with Billy, Corey had been feeling better about things, even about the bet with Cameron and the chance the Ravens wouldn't make the finals. But standing in front of that hill suddenly sent his good mood crashing down.

Even if you win the bet and the team makes the finals, what will change? asked a cold voice in his head. *You and your mum will still be scrounging to get by in that dingy little apartment, or another just like it. You'll never go anywhere. You'll never be anything.*

Corey stared hard at the hill. Like the path ahead, his life seemed unconquerable.

But I have to try, he told himself.

He picked up the handle of the cart and started walking. A quarter of the way, the muscles in his arm began to ache. Beads of sweat covered his forehead. He swapped arms, wiped the sweat off his brow with the back of his hand and kept going.

Up.

The hill got steeper. The top looked further than ever. But he kept going, one step at a time. At halfway, his legs felt like lead. His other arm was burning now. He stopped and punched at the muscles in his legs. Corey then put both hands on the cart handle, turned around and began walking backwards up the hill.

Up.

Just when he thought he was going to make it, he tripped on a pothole. His sweaty palms lost their grip, and Corey watched the cart plummet back down the hill, its handle scraping the road, catalogues flying everywhere. Finally, it came to rest near the bottom.

That's it, I give up! No more catalogues! No more footy! No more anything!

He looked at the trail of catalogues scattered down the hill. 'You can stay there for all I care,' he said.

Then he thought about his mum. She wouldn't have given up. She never gave up, no matter how bad things seemed.

Then it occurred to him. His mum was like one of those great footy players. She was selfless. And he knew what he had to do.

Corey got up and walked back down the hill, collecting the catalogues as he went. When he got to the cart, he picked it up, dusted it off and loaded it with catalogues.

Taking a deep breath, he started up the hill again.

He didn't stop climbing till he reached the top.

On the Saturday morning of the final round, Corey was woken by the sound of the telephone. Bleary-eyed, he made his way to the kitchen. His mum was already up.

'Who was on the phone?' he asked, rubbing the sleep from his eyes.

His mum looked up and smiled. 'Coach Steve. He was just confirming he'd be here at seven-thirty to pick you up.'

'Oh, right.'

'I asked him if I could tag along,' his mum said brightly. 'Don't want to miss the last game of the season.'

'You're coming?' asked Corey, suddenly wide awake.

'Is that okay?'

Corey thought about his bet with Cameron, then he looked at his mum's hopeful face. 'Sure, great.'

An hour later, Coach Steve pulled up outside the apartment.

'Thanks again for the lift to the game,' said Corey's mum, as they climbed into the dusty station wagon.

'No worries,' said Coach Steve. 'How's it all going, anyway? Still working at Crazee Bargains?'

'Oh, yes,' replied his mum. 'Every hour I can get. In fact, I've just been offered the Assistant Manager position.'

'Congratulations!' said Coach Steve.

'What? Mum, you didn't tell me that!' said Corey.

'Sorry, I only just found out yesterday and then I was so pooped when I got home it slipped my mind,' his mum said.

'That's really great,' said Corey.

Corey's mum grinned. 'Thanks, love. It's a little extra money, too, so maybe we can finally say goodbye to those cattle-dogs!'

'Cattledogs?' asked Coach Steve. 'What cattledogs?'

Corey and his mum burst into giggles. *Maybe things are looking up*, thought Corey.

But when they arrived at the homeground of the Mount Macquarie Lions, his good mood quickly evaporated.

'Judgement day!' said Cameron, as the team got ready in the change sheds. His smirk was back and worse than ever. 'Can't wait to ride those Big Wave slides with my annual pass!'

'No chance,' said Corey. But he felt that jelly wobbling inside his stomach again.

His confidence didn't improve when Coach Steve called him over. 'Corey, can we have a quick chat, mate?'

Corey was only eleven, but he knew that when someone called you 'mate' and asked to have a quick chat, it was rarely good news. He was right to be worried.

16 COREY PUTS HIS HAND UP

Corey sat on the sideline and watched as the rest of the Ravens ran up in a line to meet the Lions' attack. The team looked tired. It was the Lions' third set of six in a row. The score was locked at 6–6. It was a do-or-die game, and with five minutes before half-time, the Ravens were flatlining.

Corey was fuming inside. How could Coach Steve bench him in the last game of the season when his team needed him?

Do they need me? he wondered. *Of course*

they do. Josh has taken my place in the centre and Ravi is playing on the wing – what sort of backline is that? It's a miracle the Lions aren't ahead by twenty.

They seem to be doing okay, said the other voice in his head. *Are you worried about the team losing or about losing the bet with Cameron?*

Corey pushed the thought aside, only to be confronted by another troubling question.

Why did Coach bench me?

'I want to try Ravi in the first half today. Let's see how he handles it,' Coach Steve had said when he told Corey he'd be starting on the bench.

But why me? It was usually one of the wingers or the forwards who sat out the second half when Ravi came on.

Well, it's not like you've been playing your best lately, said the other voice sharply. It was starting to sound like Cameron.

Corey thought back to what Billy had said. *Did it really matter if he lost the bet if it meant the team could make the finals?*

The thought popped like a balloon when one of the Lions forwards burst through a tackle and lunged for the tryline. Despite Poppa's best efforts, the Lions player still managed to stretch his arm out and slam the ball down over the line. The Lions were now in the lead.

When the half-time whistle blew, the Ravens gathered in a huddle of tired bodies, sucking in air and water and orange quarters. Corey sat off to the side, still stinging from having to sit out the first half. He knew Coach had to put him on for the second half, but it felt like it was too late.

Coach Steve cleared his throat and waited for silence. 'Well, lads, it's the last game of the season. You've played well. I know you've all tried your best, but we're down 12–6 and those Lions are looking hungry. They're playing for pride. They want to end the year as winners, and we just look . . . tired. I guess we're not going to get there this time.' He paused, frowning. 'Ravens, our season is over.'

The boys looked around at each other, confused. This wasn't the Coach they knew. Coach didn't give up. Ever. If Coach had given up, what chance did they have?

Coach Steve lifted his eyes ever so slightly. 'Unless,' he said quietly, with one eyebrow raised, 'one of you has something left in the tank. Something left to give the team.' His voice grew louder. 'Unless one of you boys has the energy to put his hand up and say they have more to give!'

Corey didn't hesitate. His arm shot straight up in the air and he shouted, 'I do, Coach. I still have more to give!'

The other boys giggled, and Corey realised that maybe Coach didn't mean to literally put a hand up. Everyone was looking at him, and Corey's arm began to wilt.

Coach Steve nodded slowly and gave Corey a big, beaming grin. 'That's the spirit. Anyone else?'

Liam put his hand up next. Then Azza and Poppa. Then Blake and Tai, Josh and Junior, until everyone's hand was up in the air. Cameron looked over at Corey and smiled – not a smirk but a real smile.

'That's what I'm talking about,' said Coach Steve. He raised one hand and then the other. 'Do it with me, boys,' he said.

And the whole team put their hands together and, in one voice, screamed, 'Ravens FLY!'

Their season wasn't over yet.

From the kick-off for the second half, the Ravens Under 11s played like a different team. And Corey Wilson was like a different player.

As they waited to receive the ball, Corey no longer cared about the bet. If Cameron won, he would buy him the Big Wave Annual Pass, even if it meant that he'd have to deliver catalogues all spring and summer. He didn't even care if he never scored a try again. What was the point if no one on the team could stand playing with him? What was the point if he was angry and miserable?

As the ball spiralled towards him, Corey suddenly felt free. He didn't have to be angry. He could choose not to be. He didn't know if he could change everything. He was still Corey, after all. Smart-alec comments and cutting put-downs were second nature to him. But he knew it all started with this first touch of the footy. This first run.

He caught the ball on the full and launched himself at the Lions' defence. He sidestepped one defender, then another. He palmed off a would-be tackler who was sizing up his legs. He tore loose from another tackler who grabbed at his arm. And then he emerged into clear space.

Turbo time!

Corey was away. Legs pounding. Heart thumping. Blood rushing to his head. The cover defence was closing in. The Lions fullback was zooming towards him. Corey knew he had to time it perfectly.

Show.

He got his hands ready for the fake inside pass, then waited until the fullback was on him, reaching out to make the tackle.

And go.

Corey switched to his right and fired a perfect short pass to Josh, who was waiting on the wing – an instant before the fullback slammed Corey to the ground. Corey looked up to see Josh streak away towards the line.

‘Go!’ he shouted. Corey watched Josh outpace the chasing Lions, before diving over the line. The Ravens had scored from the kick-off.

Liam converted the goal to make it 12–12, but the Ravens were just getting started. And so was Corey.

He couldn’t believe how good it felt to give. It was amazing. He made break after break, and each time he managed to find someone else to off-load to. The rest of the team had gone up a gear as well. Junior was making his trademark cannon-ball runs before getting away a clever pass to a supporting player. Sometimes it was to another forward, sometimes it was a back. The Miller twins were combining for a second-phase play that Tai quickly dubbed 'The Michael Jackson Thriller'. Liam and Blake were executing some daring round-around set plays, which sometimes worked in training but rarely worked on the field. Somehow, today they were coming off.

The team was playing as one. Everyone was backing up, waiting for the off-load, looking for the ball. Everyone wanted to be involved. Everyone had their hand up.

After just fifteen minutes, the Ravens had blitzed the Lions on the scoreboard. It was 32–12. Corey had even scored one of those tries, as did Cameron. The two boys were still tied for top try-scorer. The final play of the game would decide the bet.

While the Ravens were well on top, they

were having too much fun to stop now. With only a few minutes left on the clock, and with one tackle remaining in their set of six, Liam called the play. 'Hot Potato!' he yelled.

Corey nodded. They were a long way out from the tryline, but Liam wanted to see if they could score one more. Corey wanted to help him.

The Ravens moved up in a diagonal line and began passing the ball – quick hands, just like at training. Each time it looked like one of the Ravens would be tackled, they managed to off-load it. Soon, they were throwing all sorts of passes just to keep the ball alive – flick passes, grenade passes, basketball dunks. The Lions could hardly keep up, and Corey was in the thick of it.

His legs were cramping. His body was exhausted. But he kept going. *Don't stop*, he told himself. *Keep backing up.*

On his fourth touch of the ball, just when it looked like the Ravens had run out of options, Corey dummied without thinking, then stepped off his right. The tired Lions defenders fell for it. Corey slipped through a hole once more. But as he sprinted towards the line, he could feel himself slowing. His lungs were on fire. His legs were like lead. He had nothing left.

I can probably make it. Maybe.

The defenders were closing in.

Then a familiar voice rang in his ear.

'Corey, I'm open.' It was Cameron.

I can keep running. I could still make it and win the bet . . . Or I could just take the tackle. We don't even need this try. We've already won, he thought. But there was only one option. He had come too far for anything else.

Corey passed the ball.

Cameron scored in the corner, bringing the score to 36–12. As the Ravens swarmed Cameron, Liam lifted Corey to his feet and then ruffled his hair so hard he almost knocked Corey to the ground again. 'Nice work, Corey!' he said. 'That was the try of the year!'

'Thanks,' said Corey. 'It felt good.'

And he meant it.

WHR

18 KEEPING THE DREAM ALIVE

'I guess you won the bet,' Corey said to Cameron as they left the field. 'I'll get you that pass to Big Wave, it just may take me a while.'

Cameron shook his head. 'I wouldn't have scored the last try if you hadn't gifted me that pass. It was a team try. It doesn't matter who put the ball down.'

'Yeah, but a bet's a bet,' said Corey.

'Really, let's forget it. My dad will probably just buy one for me, anyway.

That's all he does since he's moved out,' said Cameron. His grin disappeared. 'My mum and him don't get on.'

Corey was surprised. Cameron's life had looked so perfect that day, from behind the hedge. 'My mum and dad aren't together, either. It's a bit . . .'

'Sucky?'

Corey laughed. 'Yeah, sucky.'

'You're all right, Wilson,' Cameron said with a smile.

'Well, don't think this means I'm not going to score more tries than you next season!' said Corey.

'We still may make the finals.'

'Double or nothing?'

'That would make two passes?'

'One for you and one for your sister.' Corey grinned.

'You're on!'

Laughing, Cameron and Corey shook hands. When they got to the sideline, Corey looked around for his mum but found another familiar face instead. Billy, who was talking with Coach Steve, waved Corey over.

'Good game, Corey. You really helped turn things around out there,' said Billy.

'Thanks. I didn't realise you were coming to the game.'

'I couldn't miss the last round, could I?'

'And after that scoreline, we should go through to the finals,' added Coach Steve. 'We're keeping the dream alive.

We may even beat the Destroyers,' he said, winking at Corey.

But there was something that was still bothering Corey. 'Coach, can I ask you something?'

'Sure, Corey. What's up?'

'Why did you bench me for the first half?'

'Ah, that,' said Coach Steve. 'Well, you haven't had the best form lately. I thought sitting out a half might fire you up.'

Corey thought about it for a moment. 'I guess it did,' he said.

Coach shrugged. 'I have my moments.'

'There you are, my little warrior. You made me proud out there today!'

Before Corey could stop her, his mum

was hugging and kissing him. 'Mum, not in front of Billy,' Corey said with a groan.

Billy laughed. 'Don't worry, my mum does the same thing.'

'Mum,' said Corey, 'even though you've been made assistant manager, I still want to keep delivering the cattledogs. You know, to help out.'

His mum raised an eyebrow and grinned. 'Who are you and what have you done with my son?'

'Mum, I'm serious,' said Corey. 'You get what you give, you know? I plan on giving a whole lot more from now on.'

Billy gave him a wink. 'Wise words. I'll have to write that down.' He turned to Coach Steve and whispered, 'Cattledogs?'

‘Best not to ask,’ said Coach Steve.

Billy nodded.

Corey stood there feeling tired but at one with the world. It was like he’d finally made it to the top of that hill. And the view was well worth the climb.

1. Fullback: Cameron 'C. C.' Cotter
2. Winger: Nick Raco
3. Centre: Blake 'The Fake' Vargas
4. Centre: Corey Wilson
5. Winger: Josh Brown
6. Five-Eighth: Tai Nguyen
7. Halfback: Liam McGill
8. Prop Forward: Junior 'Cannonball' Taafuli
9. Hooker: Ahmed 'Azza' Azzi
10. Prop Forward: Lucas 'Poppa' Popovic
11. Second Row: Matthew 'Michael' Miller
12. Second Row: Jackson Miller
13. Lock Forward: Jack Monroe

Reserve: Ravi Rangarajan

Coach: Steve Smith

AGE: 11 WEIGHT: 45 kg

HEIGHT: 152 cm POSITION: Centre

Corey's motormouth may get him into a bit of trouble with his teammates, but this fiery centre is the team's speed demon. Corey is a deadset try machine with a killer sidestep, although he does have a tendency to go 'one out' a little too often.

Besides playing footy, Corey helps his mum make ends meet by delivering Crazee Bargains catalogues. He's pretty handy on a skateboard as well.

AGE: 10

HEIGHT: 160 cm

WEIGHT: 59 kg

POSITION: Prop Forward

Junior is the youngest player on the team, and he is also the biggest. His tackle-busting line breaks have earned him the nickname Cannonball. But don't be fooled by his size. This forward has some pretty handy ball skills and a tricky little flick pass, too. Junior can win a game almost single-handedly, but prefers to throw the ball around with his teammates and rely on his skill, rather than his size. When he's not breaking tackles, this unlikely rapper is busting rhymes. Word!

AGE: 10

HEIGHT: 145 cm

WEIGHT: 42 kg

POSITION: Winger

An inexperienced but speedy player, what Josh lacks in confidence and size, he makes up for in heart. Josh is a great support player and, given a chance, he will tear away down the sideline. Expect lots of points from this galloping winger before the season is over – once he gets his ball-handling under control.

Josh's interests include football and his fave food is a classic barbecued sausage sandwich – don't forget the tomato sauce.

Ravi is super-smart and can rattle off any footy statistic or piece of trivia about the game you can throw at him. Just don't throw him the football – his skills are a little on the under-developed side. But with a little confidence and coaching, Ravi's natural intelligence and enthusiasm for footy may convert to points on the board before the season ends.

Ravi is a self-confessed maths geek and prides himself on knowing more footy facts than a TV commentary team.

AGE: 10

HEIGHT: 147 cm

WEIGHT: 41 kg

POSITION: Reserve

He might be the team's smallest player but this pocket rocket half is the Ravens' engine. Without Liam calling the plays and driving his teammates forward, the Ravens would get nowhere. His lightning reflexes and natural instinct for the game make Liam the Ravens' MVP – most valuable player.

Liam's interests include footy, footy and more footy.

AGE: 11

HEIGHT: 140 cm

WEIGHT: 38 kg

POSITION: Halfback and Team Captain

Sidestepping

Sidestepping is a great skill to have in rugby league. It can help the attacking player evade the opposition and break through the line. The trick is to make the opposition think you are going one way and then go the other, wrong-footing the defender. Like many skills in rugby league, it takes agility, speed and timing to get it right.

Key points

- As you run the ball up to the opposition, look for gaps or weaknesses in the defensive line that you can take advantage of, such as a distracted player or a player who is out of position.
- When you approach the player, step onto your outside leg, planting it in the opposite direction that you want to head towards.
- Quickly push off your outside leg, heading in the opposite direction. This should allow you to catch the defender off-balance and dodge their tackle.
- Remember, a good sidestep is about deception and evasion. Use your body movements to fool the defender into following you in one direction, then use a sudden burst of speed

to go the opposite way. But don't do overuse this tactic, otherwise the opposition will start 'reading' your step and it won't be as effective.

Support play and teamwork

Rugby league is a team sport, and being a good team player is the most important quality a footballer can have. Without teamwork, it's very hard to be successful on the footy field. In attack, that means good supporting play. If a player makes a break, he needs his teammates to back him up so the play can continue. Knowing when to pass the ball and when to hold onto it is also an important skill to develop. Timing the pass right can mean the difference between beating the defence and getting tackled.

Key points

- Always pay attention to what is happening on the field. Stay in position in the line of attack and run up with the team so you're never too far away from the action to get involved.
- If a player makes a break and you are nearby, call for the ball. Stay behind the ball carrier to avoid the chance of a forward pass.
- As the ball carrier, keep an eye on where your teammates are. Look around you for support so that you can weigh up your options quickly and get a pass away without having to slow down the play. Quick passing can help to create an overlap and allow for the attacking team to get past the defence.

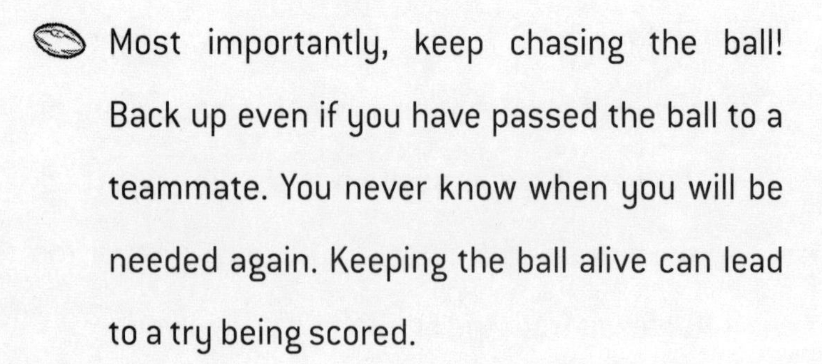

- Most importantly, keep chasing the ball! Back up even if you have passed the ball to a teammate. You never know when you will be needed again. Keeping the ball alive can lead to a try being scored.

COLLECT THE SERIES!

ALL FOUR BOOKS AVAILABLE NOW